# Prehistoric People of
# Moccasin Bend
## Chattanooga, Tennessee

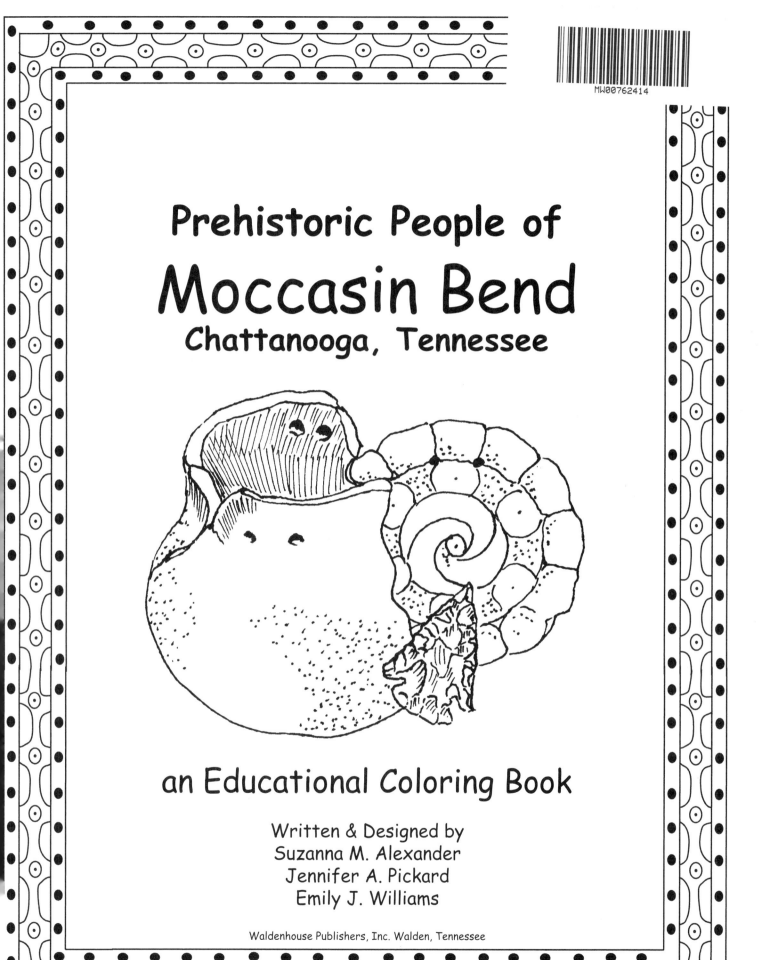

# an Educational Coloring Book

Written & Designed by
Suzanna M. Alexander
Jennifer A. Pickard
Emily J. Williams

Waldenhouse Publishers, Inc. Walden, Tennessee

## Dedication

This educational coloring book is dedicated
to the prehistoric people who cherished this bend in the river.
May we continue to preserve, protect and value
Moccasin Bend.

Illustrated by Laura Feely Ashline

The authors are grateful for the assistance and support
given by Lawrence Alexander and the staff at Alexander
Archaeological Consultants, Laura Myers, a partner in the initial
dream, and the many friends who reviewed this book and
made helpful comments.

Library of Congress Cataloging-in-Publication Data

Alexander, Suzanna M. (Suzanna May), 1942-
  Prehistoric people of Moccasin Bend, Chattanooga, Tennessee : an educational coloring book / written
& designed by Suzanna M. Alexander, Jennifer A. Pickard, Emily J. Williams.
      p. cm.
  Summary: "Describes the ways of life of prehistoric people who lived on Moccasin Bend, Chattanooga,
Tennessee. Page border designs, background information and illustrations to color are based on actual
archaeological discoveries. Includes a glossary, references, activities and field trip list"--Provided by
publisher.
  Includes bibliographical references and index.
  ISBN-13: 978-0-9779189-3-5 (alk. paper)
  ISBN-10: 0-9779189-3-9 (alk. paper)
 1.  Moccasin Bend National Historic Site (Tenn.)--Juvenile literature. 2.  Indians of North America--
Tennessee--Chattanooga--Antiquities--Juvenile literature. 3.  Paleo-Indians--Tennessee--Chattanooga
--Juvenile literature. 4.  Woodland Indians--Tennessee--Chattanooga--Antiquities--Juvenile litera-
ture. 5.  Excavations (Archaeology)--Tennessee--Chattanooga--Juvenile literature. 6.  Chattanooga
(Tenn.)--Antiquities--Juvenile literature. 7.  Coloring books--Tennessee--Chattanooga.  I. Pickard,
Jennifer A. II. Williams, Emily J. III. Title.
  E78.T3A43 2006
  976.8'82--dc22
                                        2006028459

Quantity discounts are available on bulk purchases for educational
purposes. For information please contact www.spiralquest.com

# Introduction

This book is about the prehistoric people who lived on Moccasin Bend from 12,000 B.C. to 1650 A.D. **Prehistoric** means there is no written record to tell us how these people lived or even what they called themselves. Our knowledge of the prehistory of Moccasin Bend is the result of archaeological investigations which began in 1914 and still continue today.

The drawings in this book are based on actual prehistoric objects discovered on Moccasin Bend. The page borders are designs created by prehistoric people who lived in the Tennessee River Valley. The information presented is what has been learned to date by archaeologists.

As we researched this project, our feelings of respect and admiration grew for the prehistoric inhabitants of Moccasin Bend. These early people used their creative energy not only to survive, but also to create art, to foster community and to play. As you enjoy this book we hope you sense a connectedness with the early people and the earth which sustained them.

Suzanna, Jennifer, and Emily

Border design from a gorget found in Hamilton County, TN

# Moccasin Bend

The land called Moccasin Bend is shaped like a foot or a shoe. The shape was formed by the river we now know as the Tennessee as it passed between two mountain ridges. During the Civil War, the land was called Moccasin Point. The part of the river passing the point was called The Bend.

Moccasin Bend has been inhabited by humans for roughly 14,000 years. The land presented fertile soil. The river offered fish and mussels. The hills gave stone for tools, clay for pottery, and wildlife for meat and clothing. The forests supplied wood for fires and homes. The river bluffs provided caves for protection. The wandering river encouraged travel and trade.

Protection of this land, rich in prehistoric and historic information, began in 1926. Many of its artifacts had already been taken by treasure hunters. Some artifacts have found their way to museums around the United States. Others remain with private collectors. Construction for highways and buildings also removed evidence of the past from Moccasin Bend. In an effort to preserve this site, Moccasin Bend was established as a National Historic Landmark in 1986. The National Park Service accepted Moccasin Bend as a National Archaeological District in 2004. Now Moccasin Bend is protected by U.S. Federal laws.

Border design from artifacts found at McMahon and Lick Mounds in TN

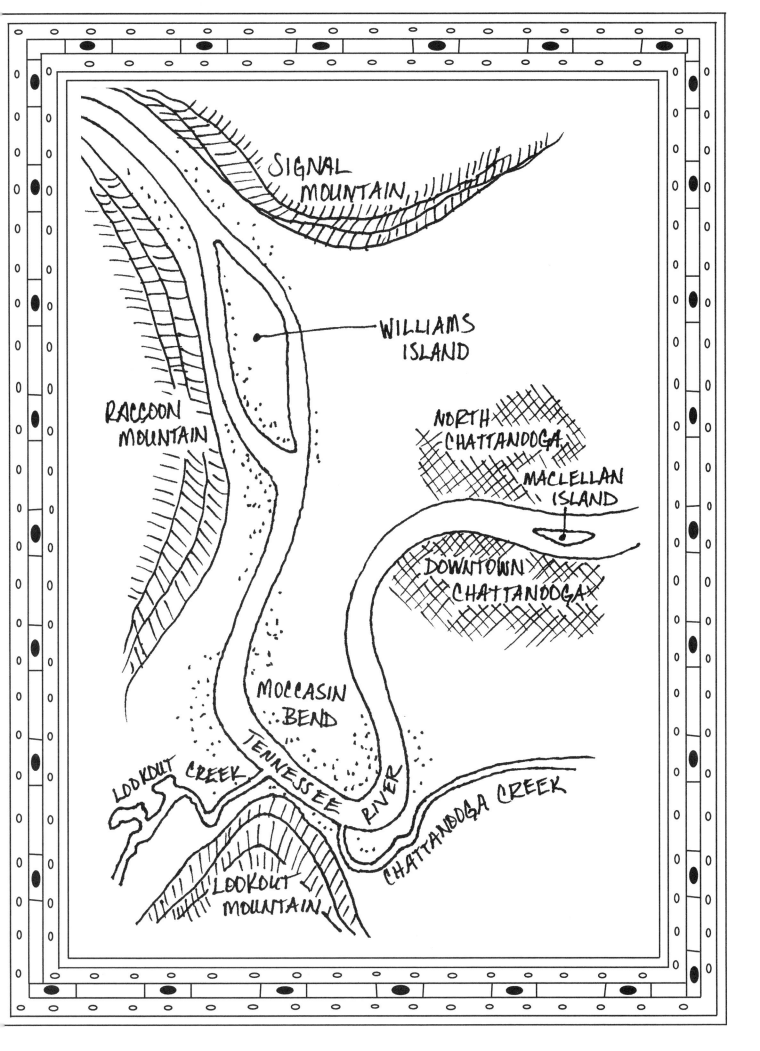

# What is Archaeology?

Moccasin Bend is a National Park Service Archaeologcial District. **Archaeology** is the study of past ways of life. **Archaeologists** are scientists who find places where ancient people lived or visited. They learn about the lives of these people from the remains of their food, tools, homes, and garbage dumps. The broken or whole objects which remain are called **artifacts**. The places where artifacts are found are called **sites**. What the people left behind as garbage, archaeologists call the **midden**.

When archaeologists first examine a site, they survey and map it. Then layers of earth are excavated and studied. **Features** such as colors of the soil may tell where houses and fires were located. Artifacts are carefully removed from the ground. They are sketched, photographed, sorted, and catalogued. The artifacts are clues. How deep they are found in the soil helps determine how old they are. Artifacts found together reveal what activities took place at the site. How people lived, worked, and played during a particular period of time is called their **culture**. Archaeologists divide prehistoric cultures into the four time periods; Paleo, Archaic, Woodland, and Mississippian, presented in this book.

Preserving, understanding, and honoring humanity's past is the work of an archaeologist.

Border design from artifacts found in Marion County, TN

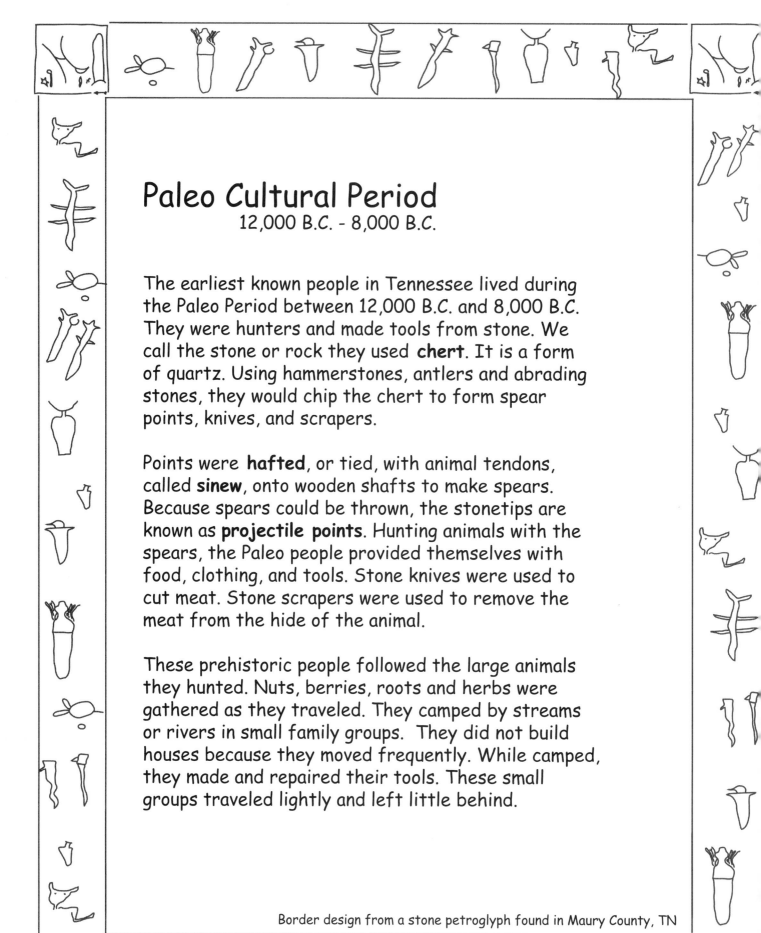

# Paleo Cultural Period
## 12,000 B.C. - 8,000 B.C.

The earliest known people in Tennessee lived during the Paleo Period between 12,000 B.C. and 8,000 B.C. They were hunters and made tools from stone. We call the stone or rock they used **chert**. It is a form of quartz. Using hammerstones, antlers and abrading stones, they would chip the chert to form spear points, knives, and scrapers.

Points were **hafted**, or tied, with animal tendons, called **sinew**, onto wooden shafts to make spears. Because spears could be thrown, the stonetips are known as **projectile points**. Hunting animals with the spears, the Paleo people provided themselves with food, clothing, and tools. Stone knives were used to cut meat. Stone scrapers were used to remove the meat from the hide of the animal.

These prehistoric people followed the large animals they hunted. Nuts, berries, roots and herbs were gathered as they traveled. They camped by streams or rivers in small family groups. They did not build houses because they moved frequently. While camped, they made and repaired their tools. These small groups traveled lightly and left little behind.

Border design from a stone petroglyph found in Maury County, TN

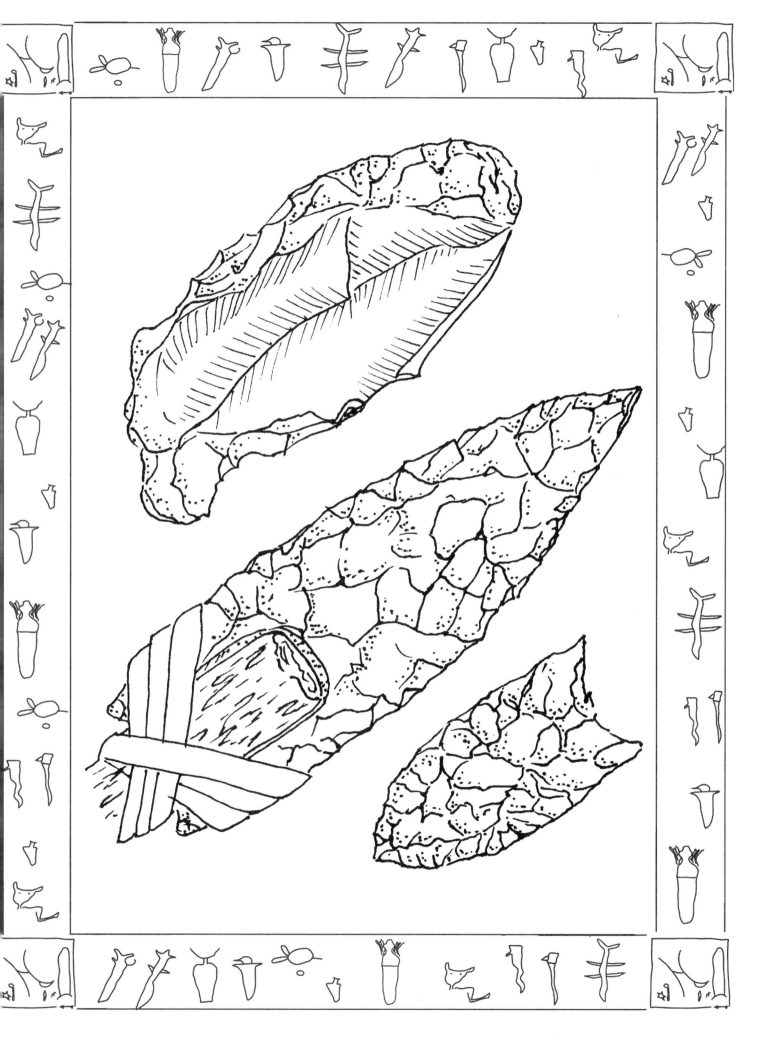

# The Archaic Cultural Period
### 8,000 B.C. - 700 B.C.

The **Archaic** people learned to gather and eat a wider variety of foods. They stayed in one place longer to collect plants, nuts, and shellfish. They left behind large piles of shells from the small, freshwater mussels they ate.

The development of a dart-thrower, or **atlatl**, increased the distance, force, and accuracy of a thrown spear. Projectile points were designed to make attachments to a shaft easier. Points made with barbs could be used to harpoon fish. **Flakes** of stone are found where the tool makers worked.

*Border design from a shell gorget found in Hamilton County, TN*

As time passed in the **Archaic** Period, the people banded together in larger family groups. The beginnings of villages were formed. Huts were made of young trees, animal hides, and bushes. Holes in animal skins were made with pointed tools of bone or stone called **awls**. To make clothing, they sewed with pieces of plant fiber or animal skin. Baskets, mats, and fish traps were woven from available plants.

Stone bowls were made out of soapstone known as **steatite** or sandstone. These soft stones were ground out with harder stone tools. Traders brought these stones from other areas. Local stones were used for cracking and grinding nuts, berries, and roots. Fire pits were dug and lined with rocks. Round rocks were heated in the fire and dropped into water to boil food. Archaeologists call these stones **fire-cracked** rocks.

Border design from pottery found in Oldtown, TN

# Woodland Cultural Period
### 700 B.C - 1000 A.D.

The **Woodland** people began to produce and store their food. They became farmers and stayed in one place to care for their crops. Land was cleared with stone axes. Holes for seeds were dug with digging sticks. Beans, squash, and gourds were planted. The crops were tended with hoes made with stones or shells. In addition to farming they continued to harvest wild plants, fish,and hunt small animals.

Villages were small. Houses were made in a circular shape. Holes were dug into the ground with stone spades for large posts to support the roof. Smaller posts outlined the house. The frame was covered with plant materials. Sometimes the plant material was covered with mud.

Long distance traders brought the villagers new plants for their gardens, copper and shells for ornaments, lead ore called **galena** for body paint, and quartz for tools.

Border design from a gorget found near Nashville, TN

The people of the **Woodland** period made cooking and storage pots out of clay. The clay was mixed with sand and crushed limestone. This kept the pot from cracking when it was heated in a fire to harden it. The use of sand and limestone with the clay is called **tempering**. Broken pottery was also crushed and reused to temper the new clay.

Clay was pinched into small pots. Ropes of rolled clay made larger, coiled pots. Designs were **incised** or scratched on the wet clay. Sometimes carved wooden paddles were used to **stamp** designs on the pots. Designs could also be **impressed** by objects such as shells and fingernails. Some pots were polished when dry with smooth stones. This is called **burnishing**. Broken pieces of pottery that archaeologists find are called **pottery sherds**.

Border design from Tennessee Valley pottery

During the end of the **Woodland** time period, the bow and arrow were developed. Bows were made from young hardwood trees. Animal tendon or plant fibers were used to make the bow string. The arrow makers straightened wood with heat and then smoothed the shafts with rock abraders. Arrows required the making of smaller points called **arrowheads**.Sinew was pounded and soaked to soften it for hafting the arrowheads securely into the notched shaft. Feathers from birds such as turkeys and eagles were split and tied to the arrows. This is called **fletching**.

Border design from Alabama River area pottery

# Mississippian Cultural Period
## 1000 A.D. - 1650 A.D.

The last prehistoric period, called **Mississippian**, was known for the development of large towns. The town or village was built around a public square. This **plaza** could be used for athletic, religious, political and social gatherings. The villages had defined social, political, and religious structures. Elaborate ritual activities and celebrations were held. Chiefs and their families became very important.

*Border design from a shell gorget found near the Cumberland River, TN*

During the early **Mississippian** cultural period, mounds of earth were built by the people. These **platform mounds** were built over many years. They were usually rectangular-shaped and had flat tops. Houses were placed on them for either ceremonial purposes or as a place for chiefs to live. A large village may have had a temple or religious mound, a political council mound and smaller mounds for the village leaders.

Homes for the people were built around the mounds. The houses were constructed of **wattle and daub**. Wattle walls were made of tree poles and woven branches. A clay plaster was daubed onto the wattle. Seats were woven into the wall. Fire pits and house floors were made of clay.

Corn, beans and squash were the predominant crops. The cornfields surrounded the villages. Some villages were protected by wooden walls, called **palisades**. Dug-out canoes were used for extensive travel up and down the river.

Border design from a shell gorget found in TN

**Mississippian** period pottery was tempered with shells and a local iron ore called **hematite**. Handles made of clay were added to the pots. Long necked bottles were made. Decorations became more elaborate as people became specialized in their roles as artists in the community. Finger markings, complicated-stamping, incised patterns and punched patterns called **punctated** developed.

Border design from TN stamped pottery

The designs created by the **Mississippian** artists included symbols representing circles, hands, eyes, crosses, suns, birds, and serpents. Stone and clay pipes were made to resemble animals. Gaming stones, beads, and ear spools were skillfully made by craftsmen. Elaborate chest decorations called **gorgets** were carved on seashells. Certain gorget designs may have defined family, political or tribal memberships.

When Europeans arrived in the Tennessee River Valley in the year 1540, they found a productive, creative, and organized civilization. By 1630, Moccasin Bend had been abandonded by prehistoric peoples.

Border design engraved on a bowl from Moundville, AL

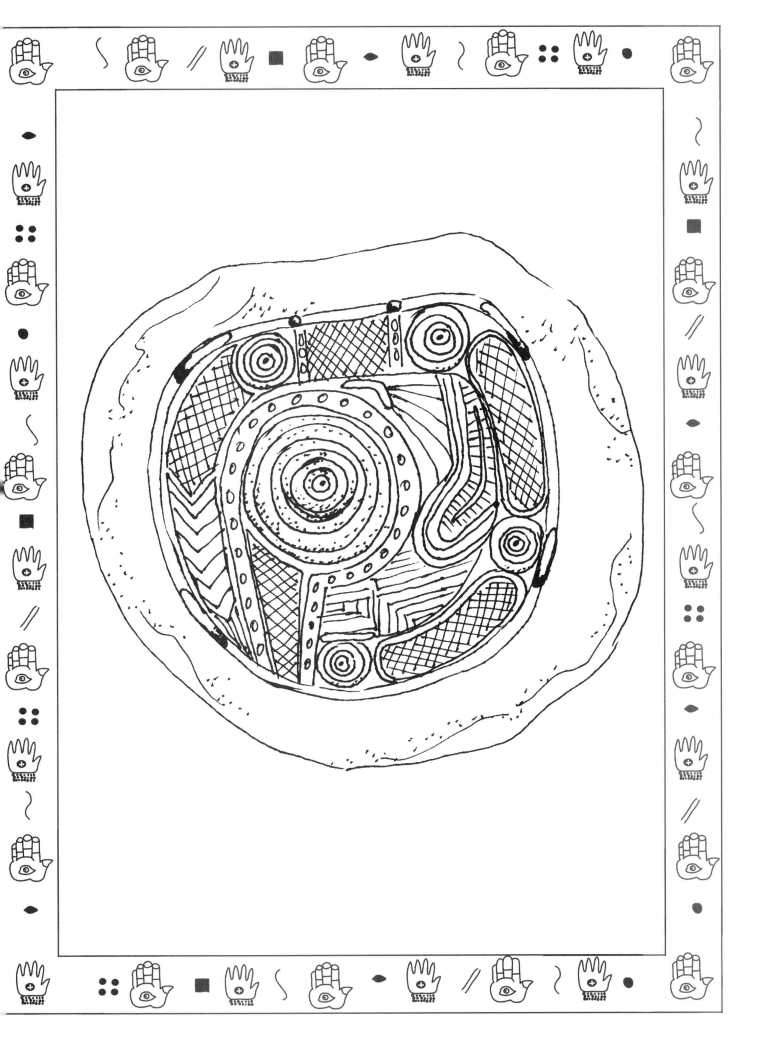

# Activities

~ Create your own border on this page and the next.
~ Sleep outside.
~ Walk in the woods.
~ Plant corn kernels with a digging stick.
~ Look for animal tracks.
~ Collect feathers.
~ Watch animals and birds.
~ Go fishing.
~ Listen to your family's stories.
~ String rocks and shells with holes for a necklace.
~ Run water through dirt and watch how a river forms the land.
~ Make a Clay Pot.
~ Grind acorns between two stones.
~ Pretend you lived 1,000 years ago.
~ Eat corn, squash, beans, and nuts.
~ Learn the stories told by the River Scenes on the outside walls of the TN Aquarium.
~ Trace the Tennessee River on a map to see how traders got to the ocean.
~ Hit sticks together and shake a dried gourd (or paper bag) filled with seeds to make music.
~ Examine your room and garbage to see what clues an archaeologist would find that would tell who you were and how you lived.

Border designed by _____

# Field Trips

~ Chattanooga Regional History Museum
  400 Chestnut Street, Chattanooga, Tennessee
  www.chattanoogahistory.com

~ Chucalissa Archaeological Museum and Village Reconstruction
  1987 Indian Village Drive, Memphis, Tennessee
  chucalissa.memphis.edu

~ Etowah Indian Mounds Historic Site
  Cartersville, Georgia
  www.gastateparks.org/info/etowah

~ Fort Loudoun
  Vonore, Tennessee
  www.fortloudoun.com

~ Frank H. McClung Museum
  University of Tennessee, Knoxville
  mcclungmuseum.utk.edu

~ Moccasin Bend Archaeological District
  Blue Blazes Trail
  www.moccasinbendpark.org

~ Moundville Archaeological Park
  Moundville, Alabama
  www.moundville.ua.edu/home.html

~ Museum of the Cherokee Indian
  Cherokee, North Carolina
  www.cherokeemuseum.org

~ Point Park on Lookout Mountain, Tennessee (to view Moccasin Bend)
  www.roadsidegeorgia.com/site/pointpark.html

~ Russell Cave National Park
  Jackson County, Alabama
  www.nps.gov/ruca

~ The Passage and the Plaza Time Lines at Ross's Landing Park
   Downtown Chattanooga, Tennessee
   www.visitchattanooga.com/tn_river_park.htm

Border designed by _____

# Time Line

## Moccasin Bend

## The World

600,000 B.C. Handaxes used in Africa
30,000 B.C. Cave art made in France
12,000 B.C. Grindstones used to make flour
           in Egypt
10,500 B.C. Pottery used in Japan

**Paleo Period/12,000-8,000 B.C.**
Noamadic Hunters
Small family groups

**Archaic Period/8,000-700 B.C.**
Hunting and gathering
Beginning of temporary settlements

6,500 B.C. Cattle domesticated in Africa
5,000 B.C. Maize and gourds cultivated in Mexico
4,500 B.C. Sails used in Mesopotamia
4,100 B.C. Sorghum and rice cultivated in Sudan
3,000 B.C. Stonehenge construction began
2,700 B.C. Earliest Egyptian pyramids built and
           silk weaving starts in China
2,200 B.C. Minoan palaces built on Crete
1750 B.C.  Bronze work in China
1337 B.C.  Egyptian King "Tut" buried

753 B.C. Rome founded
50 B.C.   Chinese silk traded to the Romans

**Woodland Period/700 B.C. - 1000 A.D.**
Beginning gardening and ceramics
Living in semi-permanent villages

0       Christian dating system begins. B.C. means
          Before Christ. A.D. means Anno Domini,
          years of the Lord
50 A.D.   Rome is the largest city in the world;
          population: 1 million
79 A.D.  Pompeii buried in Mt. Vesuvius eruption
105 A.D. Paper used in China
500 A.D.  Teotihuacan, Mexico is the 6th largest
          city in the world at 200,000 people
986 A.D. Vikings settle in Newfoundland

**Mississippian Period/1000-1650 A.D.**
Use of bow and arrow
Mound towns
Rectangular domestic structures
Widespread trade network
Palisaded villages
Intensive farming
1540 A.D. Hernando DeSoto arrived
in the area and began
the first written  history.

1000 A.D. Easter Island statues erected
1275 A.D. Marco Polo reaches China
1290 A.D. Glasses invented in Italy
1492 A.D. Columbus discovers New World
1509 A.D. Watch invented in Germany
1607 A.D. First permanent English settlement
          in America at Jamestown, Virginia
1784 A.D. Thomas Jefferson, "Father of
          Americn Archaeology" makes first
          scientific excavation in North America

Border design from a gorget found on Fain's Island, TN

# Glossary

**abrading stone**: a stone used to grind and smooth

**archaeology**: the study of past ways of life

**arrowhead**: a small sharp chipped stone tip for arrows

**artifact**: any object made or used by humans

**atlatl**: a wooden throwing attachment used to increase distance, force, and accuracy of a spear

**awl**: a hand held tool with a strong, sharp point for making holes

**burnishing**: polishing dry clay pots with smooth stones

**celt**: a stone or metal axe head

**chert**: a flint-like quartz mineral

**culture**: the shared beliefs and behaviors of a group of people

**ear spool**: large ornament worn in a person's ear lobe

**feature**: evidence of human occupation such as a fire pit or house floor that is non-transportable

**flake**: a thin chip of stone with sharp edges

**fletching**: placing feathers on an arrow to increase accuracy and distance

**flint**: a hard quartz mineral found in Dover, England

**galena**: a lead ore that was mixed with bear grease to make body paint

**gorget**: an engraved decoration or armour for protection of the throat

**haft**: to attach a handle to a tool or weapon

**hammerstone**: a stone used to remove shells from nuts or to shape stones into tools

**hematite**: iron ore

**historic**: the time period after writing could document history

**impressing**: a way to decorate pottery by pressing objects into the wet clay

**incising**: engraving pottery or shells by scratching designs with sharp objects

**mussel**: a fresh water clam with a bivalve shell

**midden**: an area used for trash disposal

**palisade**: a strong fence used for defense

**platform mound**: a manmade earthen hill created to elevate structures

**plaza**: an open area in the middle of a town used for gatherings

**prehistoric**: the time before witten history

**projectile point**: stone point used on spears or darts that were thrown

**punctating**: pottery design of dots and depressions made by a sharp object

**quartz**: a common hard mineral

**radiocardon dating**: measuring radioactive carbon to date bone, wood, charcoal and other materials

**remote sensing**: detecting hidden archaeological features at a site by passing radar or sound impulses through the ground

**sherd**: a piece of broken pottery

**sinew**: animal tendon prepared to use as cord or thread

**site**: a place where human activity occurred and artifacts were left

**stamping**: pounding designs carved onto wooden paddles into wet clay

**steatite**: a soft stone also called soapstone

**stratigraphy**: the study of layers of deposits in archaeological sites

**survey**: a systematic examination of the surface of the land

**temper**: adding things to clay to prevent pots from shrinking and cracking when heated

**wattle and daub**: construction using interwoven branches coated with clay mixtures

# References

*The History of Archaeology*, 1998
    by Maev Kennedy
    Octopus Publishing Group Limited

*Moccasin Bend National Historic Landmark:*
*Archaeological Overview and Assessment*, 2006
    Lawrence Alexander, Julie Coco, Nicholas Honerkamp,
    Bruce Coucil, & Harry Hays
    Alexander Archaeological Consultants, Inc. for the
    National Park Service

*Past Worlds: The Times Atlas of Archaeology*, 1995
    Crescent Books

*Sun Circles and Human Hands: The Southeastern Indians*
*Art and Industry*,  1957
    Edited by Emma Lila Fundaburk & Mary Douglass
    Fundaburk Foreman
    Southern Publications; Fairhope, Alabama

*The World of the Southern Indians*, 1983
    by Virginia Pounds Brown & Laurella Owens
    Beechwood Books; Birmingham, Alabama